Remember – green means *go!*

Put your pencil or crayon on the
green spot before you start to draw.

Use your crayon to draw the tracks that these
creatures have left behind.
Draw over the top of the lines.

3

More tracks and trails

Draw your own snail trail here.

See how many more tracks and trails you can make on another piece of paper.

4

Can you draw these round shapes?
Start on the green spot and follow the dotted lines.

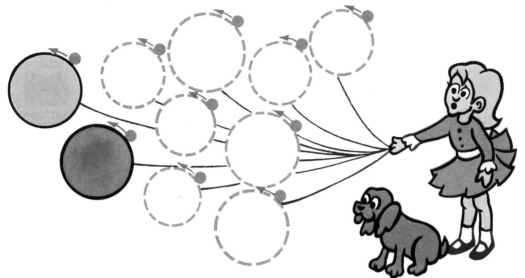

Draw the heads round these faces.

Can you draw some round shapes here?

5

Put the wheels on this train.

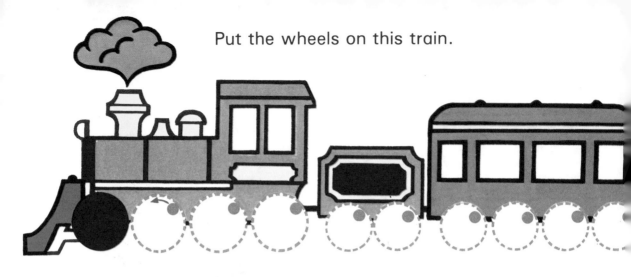

While the giant is asleep, draw the buttons on his shirt.

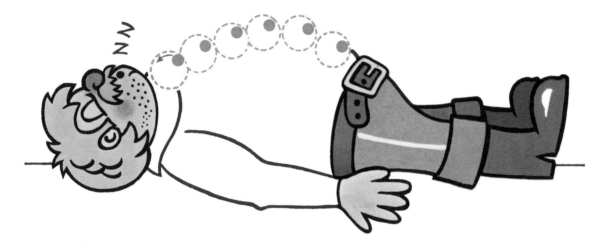

Can you draw some more oranges, balls and round buttons like these?

Help the man to paint his fence. Draw in all the posts.

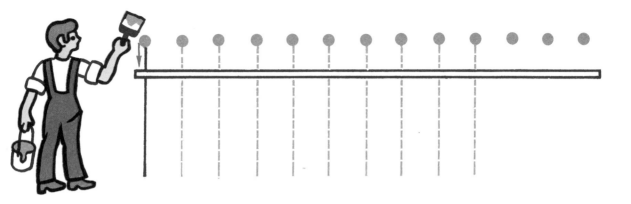

Draw the stalks on these flowers.

Draw the doors and windows on the houses.

7

Put the steps on the ladder so that the man can climb down.

Can you draw another ladder here?

Finish drawing the lion's mane.

Follow with your crayon where the ball has bounced.

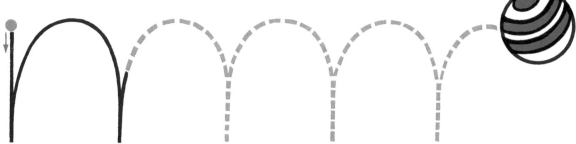

Draw the cups.

Draw the clown's teeth.

Finish drawing the teeth of the saw.

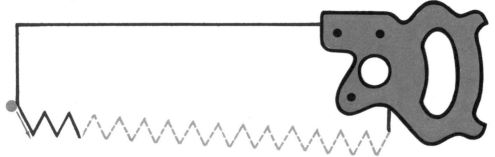

Draw the dragon's teeth.

Can you draw some more patterns like this?

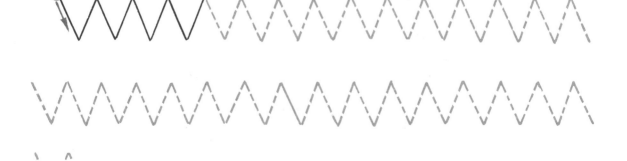

Follow where the girl has painted a pattern.

The top has made a pattern, draw where it went.

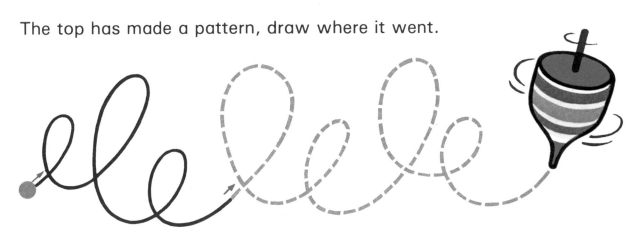

The bee is flying round and round.
Follow the bee.

Now practise these patterns

Remember not to take your crayon off the page until you have
finished each pattern or shape. Always start at the *green* spot.

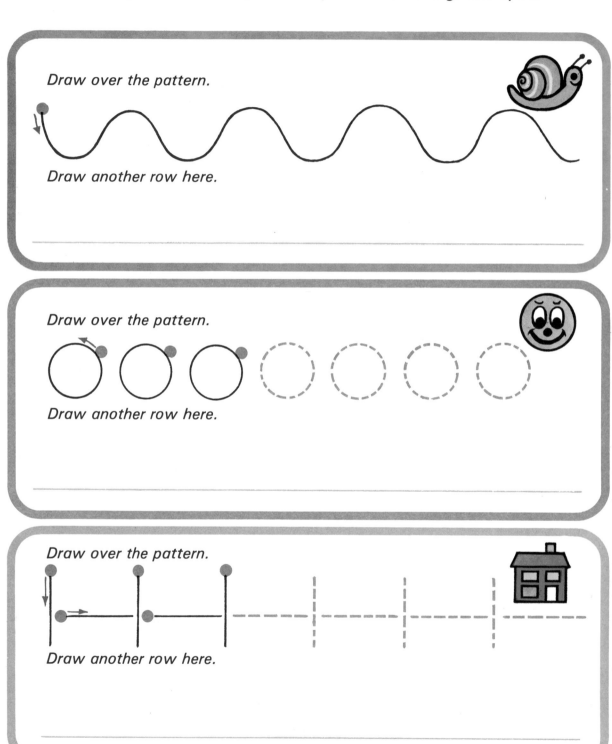

Draw over the pattern.

Draw another row here.

Draw over the pattern.

Draw another row here.

Draw over the pattern.

Draw another row here.

Draw over the pattern.

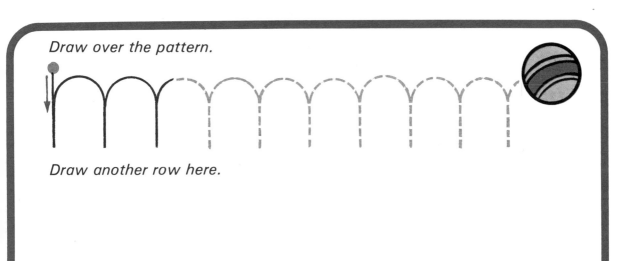

Draw another row here.

Draw over the pattern.

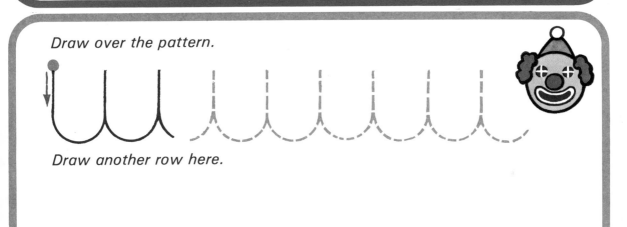

Draw another row here.

Draw over the pattern.

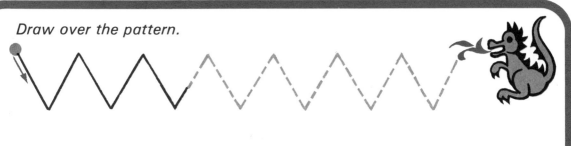

Draw another row here.

Draw over the pattern.

Draw another row here.

_____

Draw over the pattern.

Draw another row here.

_____

Draw over the pattern.

Draw another row here.

_____

Draw over the pattern.

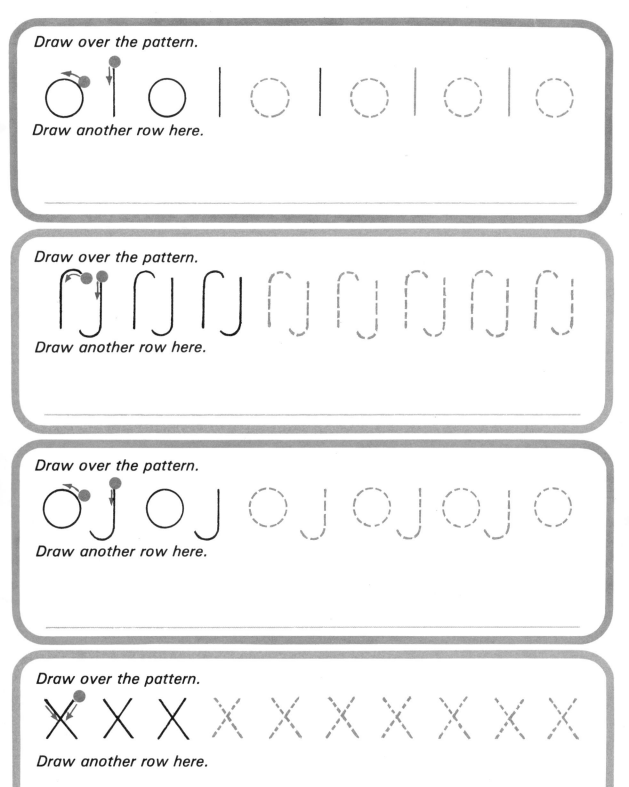

Draw another row here.

Draw over the pattern.

Draw another row here.

Draw over the pattern.

Draw another row here.

Draw over the pattern.

Draw another row here.

15

Now we can start to make letters

Find a pencil for these pages and remember
to start drawing at the *green* spot.

Draw over the letters.

C C C C C C C C

Draw over the dotted lines.

C C C C C C C C

Draw more letters here.

Draw over the letters.

O O O O O O O O

Draw over the dotted lines.

O O O O O O O O

Draw more letters here.

Draw over the letters.

a a a a a a a a

Draw over the dotted lines.

a a a a a a a a

Draw more letters here.

Draw over the letters.

Draw over the dotted lines.

Draw more letters here.

Draw over the letters.

Draw over the dotted lines.

Draw more letters here.

Draw over the letters.

Draw over the dotted lines.

Draw more letters here.

17

Draw over the letters.

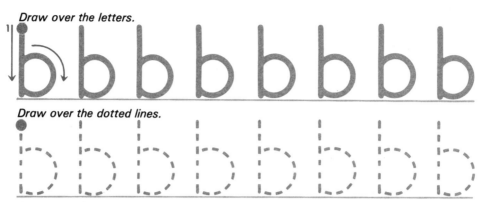

Draw over the dotted lines.

Draw more letters here.

Draw over the letters.

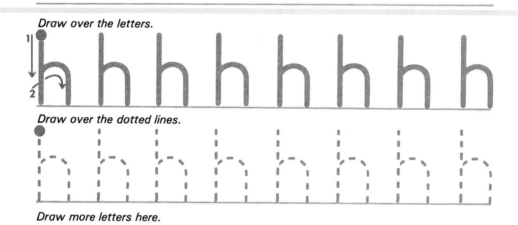

Draw over the dotted lines.

Draw more letters here.

Draw over the letters.

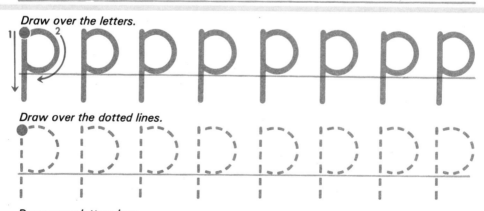

Draw over the dotted lines.

Draw more letters here.

Draw over the letters.

Draw over the dotted lines.

Draw more letters here.

Draw over the letters.

Draw over the dotted lines.

Draw more letters here.

Draw over the letters.

Draw over the dotted lines.

Draw more letters here.

Draw over the letters.

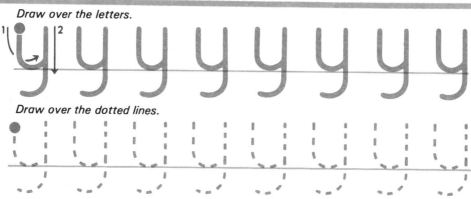

u u u u u u u

Draw over the dotted lines.

u u u u u u u u

Draw more letters here.

Draw over the letters.

y y y y y y y y

Draw over the dotted lines.

y y y y y y y y

Draw more letters here.

Draw over the letters.

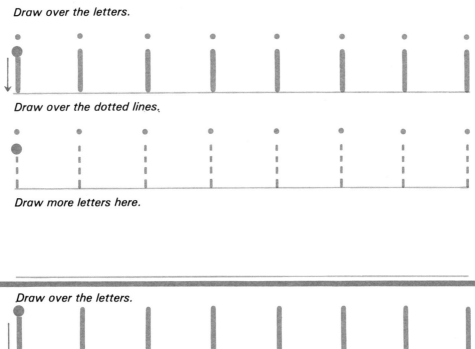

Draw over the dotted lines.

Draw more letters here.

Draw over the letters.

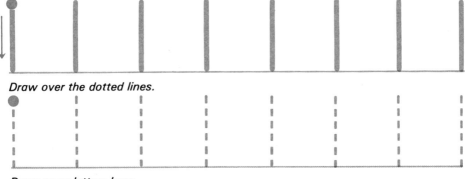

Draw over the dotted lines.

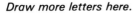

Draw more letters here.

Draw over the letters.

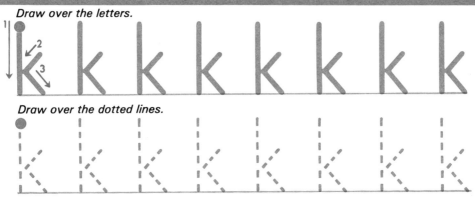

Draw over the dotted lines.

Draw more letters here.

Draw over the letters.

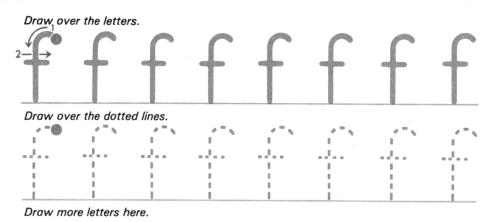

Draw over the dotted lines.

Draw more letters here.

Draw over the letters.

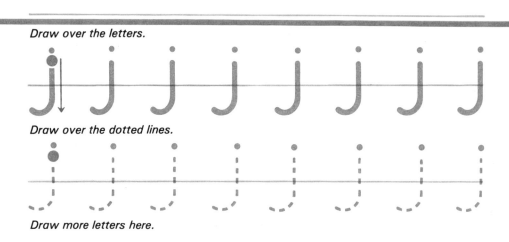

Draw over the dotted lines.

Draw more letters here.

Draw over the letters.

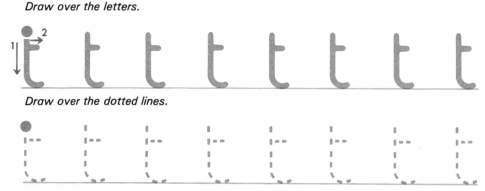

Draw over the dotted lines.

Draw more letters here.

Draw over the letters.

Draw over the dotted lines.

Draw more letters here.

Draw over the letters.

Draw over the dotted lines.

Draw more letters here.

Draw over the letters.

Draw over the dotted lines.

Draw more letters here.

Draw over the letters.

Z Z Z Z Z Z Z Z

Draw over the dotted lines.

Draw more letters here.

Draw over the letters.

e e e e e e e e

Draw over the dotted lines.

Draw more letters here.

Draw over the letters.

S S S S S S S S

Draw over the dotted lines.

Let's practise the letters again.

coacoacoacoa

You draw a row here.

dgqdgqdgqdgq

You draw a row here.

bhpbhpbhpbhp

You draw a row here.

25

nmrnmrnmrnmr

You draw a row here.

uyuyuyuyuyuyu

You draw a row here.

ilkilkilkilkilkilkilkilk

You draw a row here.

f j t f j t f j t f j t f j t f j t f j t

You draw a row here.

v w x v w x v w x v w x

You draw a row here.

z e s z e s z e s z e s z e s z e s

You draw a row here.

Here are all the letters in the right order. This is called the *alphabet.*
Practise drawing the letters underneath.

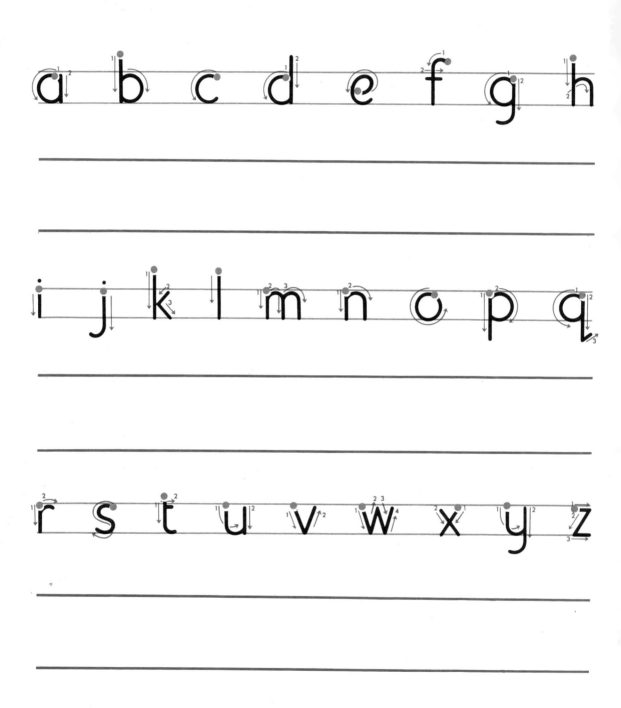

Here are the numbers. Count the things in the pictures and practise drawing the number shapes.

1 2 3 4

5 6 7

8 9 10

29

Here is the alphabet again.

These are capital letters. We mainly use these letters at the *beginning* of important words, like names.

Practise these letters underneath.

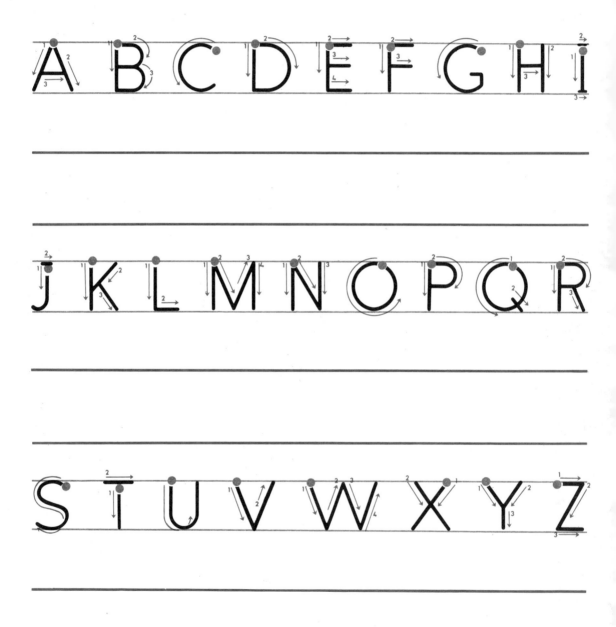